MICHAEL GARLAND

KING PUCK

HarperCollinsPublishers

Manufactured in China.

Library of Congress Cataloging-in-Publication Data is available.
ISBN 978-0-06-084809-5 (trade bdg.) — ISBN 978-0-06-084810-1 (lib. bdg.)
ISBN 978-0-06-084811-8 (pbk.)

Typography by Jeanne L. Hogle
10 11 12 13 SCP 10 9 8 7 6 5 4 3
❖
First Edition

To my grandfather,
Michael Carney

"Ah, Finny," Seamus said to his goat, "we're so lucky. Our mountain is the most beautiful in all of Ireland."

It *was* beautiful, but it was lonely. Only the wee fairies lived nearby. Seamus had no one to talk to but his goat!

At night Seamus liked to read the stories of Finn MacCool. The goat loved when the hero giant tasted the magic salmon and gained the gift of wisdom. Finny wanted to be wise, too. "These stories are a joy, but wouldn't some new books be wonderful?" Seamus asked. Then he sighed, wishing for an answer.

The fairies began to pity the sad farmer and his goat.
One night, while Seamus was asleep, they cast a spell.

The next morning Seamus got the shock of his life.

When he said "Good morning" to Finny, the goat said "Good morning" right back.

Then Finny said, "I'm famished. What a lovely day it is. The river is up. I wonder if the trout are biting. . . ."

"How did you learn to speak?" Seamus asked.

"I don't know," replied Finny. "Perhaps I learned from you."

Seamus was happy, but the fairies weren't finished with their plan.

Later that day the two friends discovered a handbill.

"*The King Puck Festival!* What is that?" Finny asked.

"The judges pick the best goat to crown King Puck, the only king in Ireland! It's just for one day, but it's quite an honor."

"Let's go!" cried Finny.

COME TO THE KING PUCK FESTIVAL IN KILLORGLIN

Seamus hastily packed some food and proudly
brushed Finny's hair.

"You'll be named King Puck for sure!" he exclaimed.

Happy and hopeful, they talked and walked all day
and night down the mountain path.

"Look at all those ribbons and flags," Seamus said to Finny
as they crossed the bridge into Killorglin.

"And isn't this music splendid?" Seamus remarked.
Finny clacked his hooves in time to a fancy jig.

Suddenly the music stopped as the farmers
and their grand goats entered the square.
Now feeling ordinary—and a little
foolish—Finny joined Seamus
at the end of the line.

The judges were less than impressed with Finny.
They turned to walk away when he stepped forward.
"May I please have another chance?" he asked.
"I'd like to recite the tale of Finn MacCool."

The people of Killorglin had heard the story before,
but never told by a goat.
When Finny completed the tale, the crowd went wild.
The judges had no choice. They picked Finny to be King Puck!

With great fanfare, Finny and Seamus led a
parade through the narrow streets of town.

The crowd cheered as the mayor of Killorglin placed a gold crown on Finny's head.

"I name thee King Puck, the only king in Ireland!" he proclaimed.

"King Puck, as mayor it is my pleasure to grant you one wish.
What will it be? Gold? Silver? A mountain of hay?"
Finny glanced at Seamus. He knew what they wanted the most.
"Books!" he said. "We'd like nothing more than books!"
The crowd cheered, and Finny felt as wise as Finn MacCool.

Seamus and Finny never wanted for another book or better company. Once a week Miss Margaret Mary Carney, the librarian from Killorglin, drove up the steep mountain with a fresh bag of books.

King Puck got his wish. And the fairies were happy, too.

Author's Note

Ireland is a special place for me. My roots are there. Both sets of my grandparents fled poverty in Ireland and came to America to find better lives. I enjoy visiting this vast and beautiful country. In Ireland the ancient past seems to exist side by side with the present. A new story is waiting around every bend.

I found my story in a wonderful town in the southwest of Ireland on the famous ring of Kerry. It's called Killorglin. Every year, from August 10th to 12th, people gather there to celebrate Puck Fair. This street fair has food, music, and dancing—but the high point is the crowning of a local goat chosen to be King Puck.

No one is certain of the exact origins of the custom. It may date back to the seventeenth century. One legend says a local goat saved the town by warning of an impending attack from the dreaded English oppressor Oliver Cromwell and his rotten Roundheads. Other sources say the custom dates back to pagan times. Whatever the reason, it makes for a fun celebration in a rural town that time seems to have forgotten.

Another reason I love this place so much is because of its beautiful golf course. During the summer, you can play very late, since it stays light until ten o'clock at night. For a duffer, it's paradise on earth!

My grandfather Michael Carney and my great-grandmother Margaret